KB162097

Dream Voices Wind Voices

Dream Voices Wind Voices
꿈 소리 바람 소리

인쇄 · 2014년 6월 14일 | 발행 · 2014년 6월 19일

지은이 · 신현숙
펴낸이 · 한봉숙
펴낸곳 · 푸른사상
주간 · 맹문재 | 편집 · 서주연 | 교정 · 김소영

등록 · 1999년 7월 8일 제2-2876호
주소 · 서울시 중구 충무로 29(초동) 아시아미디어타워 502호
대표전화 · 02) 2268-8706(7) | 팩시밀리 · 02) 2268-8708
이메일 · prun21c@hanmail.net / prunsasang@naver.com
홈페이지 · http://www.prun21c.com

ISBN 979-11-308-0242-8 03810

값 13,000원

Dream Voices
Wind Voices

Poem Hyon—Sook Shin
Translation (in English) Soh—jung Yoo

푸른사상
PRUNSASANG

| 꿈 소리 바람 소리를 내면서 |

지난 30여 년
한국어의 맛과 멋을 분석하면서 보냈다
때로는 마음에 드는 단어를
때로는 재미있는 속담을
때로는 새로 태어난 문학 작품을 분석하면서
짧지 않은 30여 년을 잊고 살았다

의미를 찾으려고 밤을 새우고
쓰임새를 밝히려고 시간을 보냈다

그러던 어느 날부터
살아 숨 쉬는 소리를 들으면서
지나가는 바람 소리를 들으면서
나는 새로운 꿈을 꾸었다

For the last 30 years

I have spent my time analyzing the taste and virtues of the Korean language

At times likeable words

At times enjoyable proverbs

At times while analyzing newly born literary works

I have been living in neglect of the not-so-short 30 or so years

Burning the midnight oil trying to find meaning

Consuming time in attempts to unearth a word usage

Then from one day

While listening to the living and breathing sound

While listening to the passing sound of the wind

I dreamed of a new dream

그동안 조각낸 소리를 모아
그동안 함께한 친구들에게
작지만 소중한 마음을 담아
감사편지를 쓴다

2010년 한 여름에
안산 기슭에서
신 현 숙

By collecting the pieces of sound

To the friends who have been by my side

Deep from my heart though small but precious

I write this thank-you letter

One summer day in 2010

From the shores in Ansan

Hyon-Sook Shin

제 2 부 소리따라 모양따라

Section 2 By Sound By Shape

제3부 시간과 공간을 넘어

Section 3 Beyond Time and Space

| 차례 |

제1부 Section 1

친구와 함께 *With a Friend*

친구

어여쁜 이름으로 내 가슴 속에
뜨거운 이름으로 내 머리 속에
파도처럼 일렁이는 사랑을 새기며

강렬한 눈빛으로
뜨거운 체온으로
나만의 행복을 전해 준

소꿉놀이 친구

나를 향한 살가운 눈웃음이
나를 향한 수줍은 미소가

어제도 오늘도
나를 기쁘게 한다

Friend

A sweet name in my heart
An incandescent name in my mind
A deeply entrenched love that wavers like the waves

With fiery eyes
With feverish body temperature
Bringing my very own happiness

My childhood friend

The kind smiling eyes on me
The shy smile on me

Yesterday and today
Make me happy

친구야!

수줍음에 조각난 네 마음이
번민이 가득한 내 가슴 달리고

행여 기다리는 가슴은
저무는 저녁 닮아 빨갛게 빨갛게 타들어가고

네 언어를 찾고파
숲속에 핀 보랏빛 라벤다 향을 맡는다

그러나 순수 박힌 네 얼굴은 자꾸만 부서지고
너를 잃은 빈 항아리 울림소리는
어제도 오늘도 나를 울리고
깊게 파인 외할머니 주름처럼
너를 향한 내 마음은 깊어만 간다

Hey Friend!

Your spirit in pieces by shyness
My anguish-filled heart races

By some possibility my heart sits waiting
Burning to red like the sunset

I seek to find your words
As I smell the scent of the fully bloomed purple lavender in the woods

But your face locked in purity continues to break down
The resonation of the empty earthenware jar that has lost you
Brought tears to my eyes yesterday and still does today
Like the deep wrinkles of one's maternal grandmother
My affection for you only grows deeper

자네는 변함이 없네

자네는 변함이 없네
색깔도 냄새도
그대로 익어버렸네
아마도 생각도 변하지 않았겠지
어! 눈썹은 가늘게 다듬었구만

한 잔 하세 그려
자네 푸념 소리도 들어보고
맥 빠진 내 노래도 들어보고
하나로 둘을 얻고
둘로 열을 빼앗는
영악한 젊은이처럼

지난 긴 시간
변함없는 자네와 나
길다는 것은 착각이었네
그저 변함없네 그려
자네는 언제나 변함없군 그래

You Haven't Changed

You haven't changed
In color and smell
You have ripened just that way
Presumably your thoughts haven't changed either
Wait! Your eyebrows have been thinly trimmed

Have a drink won't you
Let me hear you grumbling
And you can hear my vapid singing
Let's hatch two out of one
Vent out all the rage in a double shot
Like shrewd youngsters

Throughout all these years
The same old you and I
The passing of time was only a delusion
No change in you whatsoever
Yes you are always the same

언제나 행복한 친구

행복한 친구를 만나면
슬픔이 가득한 친구가 그립고
우울한 친구를 만나면
기쁨이 가득한 친구가 보고 싶다

그러나 꿈이 많은 친구를 만나면
언제나 행복한 친구가 생각난다

꿈이 많아 행복한 친구
행복으로 꿈을 꾸는 친구

내 마음 빼앗는 우렁찬 목소리에서
오늘도 옹골진 꿈 받아 적으며
언제나 꿈을 꾸는 친구 옆에서
내일도 행복한 친구가 된다

언제나 행복한 친구가 된다

Always a Happy Friend

When I meet a happy friend
I long for a friend full of sadness
When I meet a depressed friend
I long for a friend full of joy

But when I meet a friend full of dreams
I always think of a happy friend

A friend happy from being full of dreams
A friend who dreams out of happiness

From a sonorous voice that steals my heart
To this day I write down the substantial dreams
Always by a friend dreaming dreams
This makes a happy friend even tomorrow

This always makes a happy friend

오늘

하나의 접힘은 또 하나의 열림
깊어지는 접힘은 더 깊어지는 열림
하나에 또 하나에
엇갈리는 순간순간

아픔 하나가 열리고
기쁨이 또 하나 열리고
돌고 도는 물레 속에
감기고 또 감기는
명주실 같은 인연

접히고 열리고
팽팽 돌아가며 감기는 시간
오늘도 우리는 연인

Today

The folding of one makes for the opening of another
A deepening fold makes for a deeper opening
One after another
Crossing each other from moment to moment

A source of heartache opens
Then another source of joy opens
Around and around in a spinning wheel
Coiling and again coiling
Like the destiny of silk thread

Folding and unfolding
Time coiling round and round
Today again it is our destiny

친구에게 편지를 쓴다

1. 오늘

초록빛 바다를 사랑하고
먹구름 천둥을 무서워하는
내 친구에게 편지를 쓴다

기뻐하는 모습도
슬퍼하는 모습도 기억할 수는 없지만
그래도 친구에게 편지를 쓴다

오늘보다는 내일이
나보다는 네가
더 멋지다는
의미 없는 생각을 담아 편지를 쓴다

Writing a Letter to a Friend

1. Today

Writing a letter to a friend
Who adores the blue ocean waters
And fears black clouds and thunders

Her look of joy
Her look of sadness I can't remember
But I'm still writing a letter to this friend

I write this thoughtless letter
As I think about how you compare to me
More admirable
Tomorrow more so than today

2. 내일

내일은 좋아지겠지
상쾌한 기분으로
그 친구를 만날 수 있겠지
환하게 웃으면서 만날 수 있겠지

함께 웃으면서
서로 바라보면서
파도 소리 가득한 우리네 꿈을
정말 아름다운 꿈을 꾸면서
내일은 함께 배를 탈 수 있겠지

2. Tomorrow

Tomorrow should be better
With a fresh state of mind
I should be able to meet that friend
I should be able to meet wearing a bright smile

Laughing together
Looking at each other
Our dreams full of the sound of the waves
Dreaming of a truly beautiful dream
Tomorrow we should be able to ride a boat together

귀여운 사람

키는 나보다 크지만
몸무게는 나보다 무겁지만
나이는 나보다 많지만

가끔은 아이 같은 귀여운 사람

표정은 심각하고
몸짓은 깔끔하고
용서와 타협은 서툴지만

가끔은 미소 짓는 귀여운 사람

말이 많다고 짜증내지만
질문이 많다고 투덜대지만
언제나 침묵으로 눈웃음 짓는

당신은 언제나 귀여운 사람

Cute Person

Taller than I

Heavier than I

Older than I

Yet at times a person who is cute like a child

Expressions grave

Gestures sharp

And inept in forgiving and compromising

Yet at times a cute person wearing a smile

Irritated by too much talk

Disgruntled by too many questions

Yet always silently smiling with the eyes

You are always a cute person

그것도 못하냐고 타박하지만
그것도 모르냐고 핀잔주지만
가끔은 친절하게 설명하는

당신은 언제나 귀여운 사람

자유로운 시간과 공간 속에서
소중한 꿈을 찾는 귀여운 사람

언제나 소리 없이 다가오는
귀여운 사람

이제는 내 친구

Criticizing about inability

Scolding for not knowing

Yet at times cordially providing explanations

You are always a cute person

A cute person who finds precious dreams

Within the flexibility of time and space

A cute person

Always drawing near without a sound

Now a friend of mine

연인

"얼굴이 예쁘냐"고 묻는다
아니면 돌처럼 보이느냐고

동글동글한 화진포 돌보다 예쁘고
7번 도로 활짝 핀 황금색 금계국보다도 예쁘다고

엉뚱하지만 정이 가득한 대답

"사랑하냐"고 묻는다

사랑은 말로 하는 것이 아니고
몸으로 느끼는 것이라고

기대는 살짝 비켜갔지만 사랑이 가득한 대답

친구가 도반을 만났다고 한다
"도반이 뭔데"라고 했더니 정신적인 반려자라고

Lovers

"Am I pretty?" I ask
Or I ask if I look like a rock

Prettier than a round rock of Hwajinpo
Prettier than a fully bloomed golden flower along Highway 7

A crazy yet tender answer

"Do you love me?" I ask

Love is not expressed through words
But felt through the body is the answer

An answer slightly off from expectation yet still full of love

My friend says he has met a "doban"
"What is a doban?" I ask

육체적인 반려자는 애인이라고 덧붙이면서

"당신은 어디에 속하냐"고 묻는다
마음에 드는 말로 만들라고 한다
마음은 읽을 수 없지만 믿음이 가득한 대답

짧지만 정다운 연인 이야기

He replies it is a companion of a kindred spirit

While adding that a physical companion is a lover

He asks "Where do you fit in?"

Requesting for a satisfying reply

Though my feelings cannot be read a reply full of the truth

A short yet affectionate courtship story

꿈을 꾸는 친구

세월을 따라
지구 저편에서

꿈속을 헤매는 친구

안쓰러운 마음에
측은한 마음에

함께 꿈을 꾸던 친구

꿈속에서 꿈을 꾸면서
어제도 오늘도 해가 저물고

함께 꿈꾸던 내 친구는
어느새 일어나 새 친구 찾았네

나 혼자 꿈속에 남아 있네

A Dreaming Friend

Chasing time
To the opposite end of the globe

A friend roving in a dream world

With a sorry feeling
And a feeling of pity

A friend with whom I shared my dreams

As I dream in my sleep
Yesterday and today the sun grows dim

Hey my friend with whom I had shared my dreams
One day got up and found a new friend

Hey now I'm left alone in the dream

꿈속에서 또다시 꿈을 꾸네

친구 떠난 꿈속에서
친구를 찾고 있네
뱅글뱅글 돌면서 꿈 친구 찾고 있네

I'm dreaming again in my sleep

Hey in the dream where my friend has left me

I'm looking for a friend

Going around and around I'm looking for a dream friend

사랑

오늘을 사랑한다는 것은
누군가를 사랑하는 것이다

어제를 사랑한다는 것은
누군가를 사랑하는 것이다

내일을 사랑한다는 것은
누군가를 사랑하는 것이다

어제 만난 친구도
오늘 만난 친구도
내 행복의 꿈나무

내일 만날 친구도
모레 만날 친구도
내 기쁨의 꿈나무

Love

Loving today means
Being in love with someone

Loving yesterday means
Being in love with someone

Loving tomorrow means
Being in love with someone

A friend I met yesterday
A friend I met today
My dream tree of happiness

A friend to meet tomorrow
A friend to meet the day after tomorrow
My dream tree of happiness

누군가를 사랑한다는 것이
쉬운 일은 아니지만

오늘과 내일을 꿈꾸는 것은
어렵지 않은 일이다

누군가를 사랑한다는 것은
어제, 오늘, 그리고 내일을 사랑하는 것

Though loving someone

Is not easy

Dreaming about today and tomorrow

Is not a difficult task

Being in love with someone means

Loving yesterday, today, and tomorrow

인연은 아니었는데…

인연이라 생각한 두 사람

무뚝뚝한 친구에게
소중한 믿음을

인연이라 생각한 두 사람

무표정한 친구에게
진지한 사랑을

인연이라 믿은 친구는
믿음과 사랑을

인연이라 생각한 두 사람

잡은 손 뿌리치는 친구에게
수줍은 감동을

It Wasn't Destiny…

Two people who thought it was destiny

To a stone-like friend
Giving one's trust

Two people who thought it was destiny

To an emotionless friend
Giving one's committed love

The friend who believed it was destiny
Trust and love

Two people who thought it was destiny

To a friend who lets go of the held hand
A bashful emotion

인연이라 생각한 두 사람

무소식이 희소식이라는 친구에게
무한한 신뢰를

인연이라 믿은 친구는
감동과 신뢰를

그러나 그 친구 연인 있었네
두 사람 인연이 아니었네

Two people who thought it was destiny

To a friend who believed no news is good news
Limitless trust

The friend who believed it was destiny
Inspiration and trust

But that friend already had a lover
The two were not destiny

어떤 만남이

아픈 마음이
우리를 애타게 하는 어떤 만남이
슬픈 기억이
우리를 서럽게 하는 어떤 만남이

풀어도 풀어도 풀리지 않는
엉키고 엉킨 시선이
들어도 들어도 들리지 않는
차디찬 아우성이

오늘밤
자정이 넘도록
날이 새도록
서로를 그리워하며
애타게 애타게 그리워하며
달이 영글고 별이 빛나고

Some Meeting

A heart in pain

A meeting that makes us anxious

Sad memories

A meeting that makes us sorrowful

An entangled gaze tangled up

Resists disentanglement

A very cold outcry

Tonight

Past midnight

Until dawn

Yearning for each other

Yearning impatiently, impatiently

The moon is full and the stars twinkle

Another meeting in waiting

또 다른 만남이 있음을
또 다른 연인이 있음을
우리는 알지 못하네
오늘도 우리는 알지 못하네

또 다른 행복이 있음을
또 다른 사랑이 있음을
미처 알지 못하네
누구도 눈치를 채지 못하네

남은 그리움과
구겨진 안타까움이
하루를 돌아 이틀을 돌아
저만치 저만치 달려가네

Another lover in waiting

We are clueless

Till this day we are clueless

Another happiness in waiting

Another love in waiting

We are still clueless

And no one has noticed

This lingering longing

This damp regret

Circles around for a day and another

Then picks up pace bit by bit

우연

너와 나
누가 먼저 우연 길목 지나
누가 먼저 필연 길목 지나
얼굴도 생각도 닮아가는가

아픈 상처는 그대로 두고
기쁜 눈물은 그대로 두고

우연으로 말하기엔 너무 얄밉다
운명으로 말하기에 너무 차갑다

필연으로 바라는 우연을
우리에게 다가서는 운명을
하얀 지우개로 지우고 있다
싸각싸각 지우고 있다

By Chance

You and I

Who will by chance first pass the bend in the road?

Who will by necessity first pass the bend in the road?

Could our appearances and our thoughts be growing alike?

Painful scars left behind

Joyful tears left behind

Too spiteful to call it chance

Too cold-hearted to call it destiny

The chance being wished for out of necessity

The destiny coming our way

Are being washed away with a white eraser

Squeaky clean

정(情)

뜨거운 눈 밑의 정은
한 잔의 따사로운 눈물

서러운
시러운 가슴 속 열매는
호수의 무력한 배우 – 물안개

떫은 생감의 진실을
입 안 가득 깨물며 되새기는
매섭고 냉혹하게 구겨진
벗어던진 거짓 외투 속에서
아프게 부서지는 안개 속 부딪힘

거칠고 힘겨운 우리네 집짓기는
제비새끼 한 마리에 목숨을 건다

Tender Feelings

Tender feelings below the warm eyes
One cup of warm tears

Sorrowful
The fruit inside the sorrowful heart
The lake's helpless performer – wet fog

The truth of the unripe persimmon
In a mouthful is chewed over and over
In the severely and cruelly crinkled
Fake overcoat thrown away
Collides within the fog painfully giving way

Building our rugged and beleaguered home
Puts a baby swallow's life on the line

망상(妄想)

푸드득

꽁지가 빠져버렸소
장식된 깃털이 빠져버렸소

푸드득

번뜩이는 햇살에 빛을 잃었소
마지막 순간의 바램도
청아한 모시의 꿈도
빛을 잃었소

푸드득

솟구치며
얽히고 얽힌 창틀 위로
솟구치는 꿈

A Fancy

Kerplunk

The tail has fallen off
The feather ornament has fallen off

Kerplunk

Lost the light in the sparkling sunlight
Even the last-minute hope
And the pure dream of a grass cloth
Lost their luster

Kerplunk

In a rush
To the top of the coiled window frame
The rushing dream

푸드득

분노와 슬픔을 태우며
까만 연기 속에서
활활 타오르는 아름다운 망상

Kerplunk

Burning away the anger and sorrow

Inside the black smoke

Is a beautiful fancy lighting up

기약 없는 이별

구름이 가득한 하늘
육거리가 보이는 창밖

옆자리에 앉은 두 사람
마주 앉아 나누는 이야기

들릴 듯 말 듯
내 귓가에서 맴돌다
어느덧 내 귀에 들어오는 목소리

구름을 담는 마음으로
하늘을 담는 마음으로
살금살금 엿보며 담아가는 목소리

"기약 없는 이별"이란다
유행가 제목처럼

A Parting Without a Promise

The sky filled with clouds
A six-way street visible through the window

A couple sitting in the seats next to me
Sitting face-to-face sharing stories

Barely audible
Whirring around my ear
The voices then unnoticeably creep into my ear

With a heart filling the cloud
With a heart filling the sky
I cautiously fill up their voices

"A parting without a promise" they say
Like the title of a pop song

언제쯤 만날 수 있을까?
"곧 만날 수 있겠지"
유행가 가사처럼

사랑하는 마음으로 두근두근

애처로운 마음으로 살금살금

밖에서는 빗방울 소리가
찻집에선 피아노 소리가
두 사람 사이를 가로 지른다

About when would we meet next?

"It should be soon"

Like the lyrics of a pop song

With the hearts in love pounding

With a pitiful heart quietly

The sound of raindrops outside

The sound of the piano in the tea house

Cut through the couple

나귀와 아이

채찍을 든 아이
자기를 그려보듯 숭고한 돌림을 그린다

군중 속에 떨어진 왕자인 양
마냥 좋아 달리려 한다

대궐의 동과 서를 가르고
엄마의 때 묻은 무덤 위도 달려보고
친구의 동공 속을 파고들면
무척이나 상쾌한 출발이다

수평과 수직으로 시선을 모아
아이는 다시 또 채찍을 든다

시간을 넘어
공간을 넘어
제주 아이가 나귀를 탄다

A Donkey and a Child

The child holding a rod

Draws a sublime circle as if he's drawing himself

The prince sheep that fell into the crowd

Runs about aimlessly as if in reverie

Coming in between the east and the west of the royal palace

It tries running atop his mother's dirt-ridden grave

And looking deep into the pupil of a friend

It makes for a very exhilarating takeoff

Collecting the gazes side-to-side, up-and-down

The child again has a rod in hand

Beyond time

Beyond space

The talented child rides a donkey

불

태우려 한다

신의 책임 속에 구겨 들어가
인간의 의무 속에 부싯돌 그어
사각사각 서로를 부비고
부석부석 서로를 망각하며
서글픈 모순을 태우려 한다

때가 낀 할아버지 망건과
내일 살 손자의 금테 안경이
잃어버린 어제를
소리 없는 침묵으로 태우려 한다

뜨거운 불꽃 속에 피어나는 환상
빙하시대 억겁을 넘나든다

Fire

A desire to burn

Crinkling into the hands of God
Dividing the flints within man's duties
Crackling as they collide against each other
A desire to burn the sad contradiction

The old man's filthy horsehair-woven headband
And the gold-framed eyeglasses that his grandson will buy tomorrow
Are yearning to burn the lost yesterday
Into dead silence

The visions blooming inside the hot flames
Visit the perpetuity of the ice age

제2부 Section 2

소리따라 모양따라 *By Sound By Shape*

소리

굴러오는 소리
굴러가는 소리
내 가슴 속 이슬로 송글송글 맺히고
아침 햇살 속에 피어나는 맑은 목소리
단잠 깨운다

네가 굴리고
내가 받는다
내가 굴리고
네가 받는다

얼룩진 마음에 스며들고
새벽녘 귓가에 파고들고
바랜 가슴 위를
바퀴 따라 굴러가는
우리네 속삭임은
살금살금 반갑게 다가온다

Sound

The sound rolling in

The sound rolling away

Accumulate like drops of dew in my heart

The blooming crystal-clear voice in the morning sunlight

Wakes me from my sweet sleep

You roll

I receive

I roll

You receive

Our whispers

Soaked into my stained heart

Penetrated in my ear in the peak of dawn

As if rolling along on the heels of a tire

Over my washed-out heart

Stealthily and delightedly draw near

가만히 기대어 서서

가만히 기대어 서서
눈부신 하늘을
꿈꾸는 바다를
안타깝게 오늘을 그리워하며

마주 잡은 두 손을
팔랑이는 두 마음을
안타깝게 내일을 그리워하며

소리 없이
가만히 기대어 서서

투명한 미소를
따사로운 입술을

가만히 기대어 서서
상큼한 향기를 그리워한다

Standing Still Leaning

Standing still leaning
Regrettably longing for today
For the radiant sky
For the dreaming ocean

Regrettably longing for tomorrow
For our two hands clasping together
For our fluttering two hearts

Without a sound
Standing still leaning

Your transparent smile
Your warm lips

Standing still leaning
I long for your fresh scent

함성

내가 오늘 배운
크지 않은 아픔 하나는
기대를 움켜쥔 주먹

목청껏 외치는 함성을 따라
주먹은 이리저리 날아다니고
군중을 삼켜버린 함성은
절망과 고달픔을 꾸짖는다

침묵을 깨고
공허를 달리면서
함성은 하얀 앞니를 드러내며
밖으로 밖으로
와―와 터지는 고함 소리는
안타까운 고통을 부수고 있다

A Shout

What I learned today

A pain not too big

A fist grasping hope

Following the shout at the top of one's voice

The fist flies about here and there

The shout that devoured the crowd

Chides hopelessness and fatigue

Breaking the silence

Attached to a void

As the shout unveils a white front tooth

Outward outward

The rrr – rrr roaring

Is tearing up the regrettable pain

새벽

아침 열리는 소리
이슬 맺히는 소리
바람 스미는 소리

떠나간 친구 웃음소리
다가오는 친구 웃음소리

행복이 다가오는 소리
기쁨이 넘치는 소리

마주 앉은 친구의 눈웃음
기뻐하는 친구의 함박웃음

진주처럼 부서지는 아침 햇살
반짝이는 꽃 자락의 향긋한 만남

새벽의 차가운 시선

Dawn

The sound of the morning opening
The sound of the dew knotting up
The sound of the wind infiltrating through

The sound of a departed friend's laughter
The sound of an approaching friend's laughter

The sound of happiness drawing near
The sound of joy overflowing

The smiling eyes of the friend sitting face-to-face
The big smile of a delighted friend

The morning sunlight fracturing like a pearl
The fragrant meeting of the glittering flower petals

The cold glare of dawn

아침 향한 뜨거운 입술과 마주 앉아

새벽과 아침이 만나는 행복
새벽과 아침이 부딪히는 뜨거운 열정

Sitting across from warm lips facing the morning

The joy of the meeting of dawn and morning
The hot passion of dawn and morning colliding

새벽을 깨우는 빗소리

투두둑 뚝 투두둑
장맛비 소리에
새벽이 깬다

친구가 떠난다는 날
내 가슴 후려치는
장맛비 소리에 새벽이 깬다

새벽을 깨우는 빗소리에
내 머리도 내 마음도 일어나 앉아
떠나는 친구를 보내고 있다

남몰래 깨어나 소리치는 빗소리
남몰래 일어나 통곡하는 새벽

타닥 따다닥 타닥
부딪혀 떨어지는 빗소리에 새벽이 깬다

The Sound of Rain Waking Dawn

Dibble dibble dopp dopp

With the sound of the monsoon rain

Dawn awakes

The day my friend announced her leaving

My thrashing heart

With the sound of the monsoon rain dawn awakes

With the sound of the rain awaking dawn

My mind and my heart rise up sitting

Bidding farewell to my friend

The rain that awoke stealthily shouts away

The wailing dawn that awoke secretly

Plip plip ploop ploop

Dawn awakes in the colliding raindrops

오늘은 친구가 떠나는 날

새벽을 깨우는 빗소리에
새벽잠 많은 친구 생각에
잠이 없는 하루를 시작한다

Today is the day of my friend's departure

With the sound of the rain awaking dawn
In the thought of my sleepyhead friend
I start my sleepless day

바람 소리

밤을 깨우는 산바람 소리에
새벽을 깨우는 파도 소리에

어제도 오늘도 일어나

멀리 있는 친구
옆집 사는 친구
그 옛날
함께 놀던 친구 생각을 하면서
오늘 만날 친구를 그리워한다

세차게 불어오는 산바람 소리에
창문을 뒤흔드는 비바람 소리에
저 바다 저 편에서 불어오는 밤바람 소리에

잠이 깨어 일어나 앉는다

Sound of the Wind

In the sound of the mountain wind that wakes up the night

In the sound of the waves that wakes up dawn

Yesterday and today I awake

My friend at a distance

My friend living in the next house

The days of old

Thinking about a childhood friend

I long for the friend I am meeting today

In the sound of the lashing mountain winds

In the sound of the wet winds rattling the windows

In the sound of the evening winds blowing in from that ocean

from the other side

Awake from my sleep I get up and sit

싱그러운 바람을
상쾌한 바람 소리를 꿈꾸며

창을 열고 바다를 본다
창을 열고 하늘을 본다

스러지는 별
피어나는 아침

산바람 소리가 자고
파도 소리도 자고
나를 깨우던 친구 생각도
잠이 든다

Dreaming about the sound of a cool breeze

And fresh winds

I open the window and look at the ocean

I open the window and look at the sky

A collapsing star

A blooming morning

The mountain winds asleep

The sound of the waves also asleep

The thoughts of my friend that would wake me

Fall asleep as well

대금 소리를 들으며

모래 위를 지나
바다를 지나
멀리 더 멀리
내 가슴 속으로
밀려오는 친구의 대금 소리

둔탁한 소리가
멍 뚫린 대금 소리가

굵은 손가락 따라
멀리 저 멀리 날아간다

옆으로 고쳐 쥐는 양 손을 타고
옛 친구 얼굴이 보이고

하나씩 하나씩 짚어가는
두 손을 타고

Listening to the Sound of the *Daegeum**

Passing the top of the sand

Passing the ocean

Far away and farther away

Into my heart

The gush of the sound of my friend's *daegeum*

The thick sound

The hollow grave sound of *the daegeum*

Flies away far far away

Following the thick fingers

Riding the two hands clasped to the side

I see the face of an old friend

Riding the two hands

That make a grip one by one

어제 만난 친구 노래가 들리고

감은 눈 사이로
잠깐 씩 열리는 입술 사이로
호젓한 대금 소리가

점잖게 사뿐하게 내려앉는 밤

대금 소리를 들으며
시간을 잊은 채 졸고 있다

I hear the singing of the friend I met yesterday

Between the eyes closed shut
Between the intermittently opening lips
The solitary sound of the *daegeum*

Evening drawing near in a stately gentle manner

Listening to the sound of the *daegeum*
I doze away unaware of the time

* The *daegeum* is a large bamboo transverse flute used in traditional Korean music.

편지

계절로 수놓은 꽃수레에
기쁘게 실려 가는 가나다라마바사

오색 꽃잎이
눈동자 되어
초롱초롱 가슴 속 신비를 터뜨린다

파도치는 꽃물결에
기쁘게 춤을 추는 한마디 한마디

꽃잎을 엮어 수레 만들고
수레를 굴리며 디칵디칵 까르르르

꿈속을 지나가는 큰 발자국
꿈속을 달려가는 수레바퀴
점점 더 높이 점점 더 멀리
날개가 되어 날개가 되어
까만 눈동자를 찾는다

Letter

On the floriated carriage imprinted by seasonal patterns
ABCDEFG are joyfully carried away

The multi-colored petal
Becomes the pupil of an eye
And pops the scintillating mystery of the heart

On the rolling flower waves
Each and every word joyfully dancing

Making a carriage by weaving flower petals
The carriage rolls on then kaaapooooom screeeeech

The large footprint passing through the dream
The carriage wheel chasing the dream
Gradually higher gradually farther away
Becomes a wing becomes a wing
And finds a black pupil

삼베 이불을 덮고

한 여름 삼베 이불을 덮고
파각파각 소리 나는 삼베 이불을 덮고
오색 꽃 그려진 이불을 덮고

할아버지 삼베 적삼
이어붙인 할머니 앞치마
엄마의 하얀 모시저고리
아빠의 옥빛 두루마기를 그리워한다

한 여름 밥상 덮은 삼베 조각 사이로
삐져나온 풋고추 꼭지가 보이고
엄마가 만들어 준 모시 남방 속으로
일곱 살 어린 속살이 보이고

한 여름 삼베 이불을 덮고
포송포송 모양 나는 삼베 이불을 덮고
행복한 어린 시절 꿈꾸고 있다

Covered with a Linen Blanket

One summer day under a linen blanket

Under the rustling linen blanket

Under a blanket adorned with a colorful flower

I long for

Grandpa's unlined linen jacket

Grandma's patchy apron

Mom's ramie jacket

Dad's jade-colored Korean topcoat

One summer day between the table-top linen cloth

I see the protruding stem of a hot pepper

Through the ramie shirt mom had made me

I see my flesh from when I was seven years old

One summer day under a linen blanket

Under a fresh linen blanket

I dream about my happy childhood years

카드를 받고

카드 속 이야기
크리스마스카드 속 이야기

눈 쌓인 숲 속 지나
눈 쌓인 수평선 지나

아득한 지평선 보이고
신비의 종소리 들리고

행복한 웃음소리
정겨운 목소리

반짝이는 이야기 되어
작은 아이 소망이

한 송이 눈꽃으로 피어나
도란도란 모닥불 피우며

Upon Receiving a Card

The story inside a card
The story inside a Christmas card

Past the snow-blanketed forest
Past the snow-blanketed horizon

I see the distant skyline
I hear the sound of a mystical bell

The sound of joyful cheer
The nostalgic voice

Become a sparkling story
The wish of a small child

Blooms into a snowflake
Making a bonfire in affectionate whispers

이야기 가득한 카드
내가 받은 크리스마스카드

A card brimming with stories

The Christmas card given to me

너무나 작은 핑크

너무나 작은 핑크

푸른 잔디 속으로 살며시 숨어
가만히 사알짝 도르르 굴러가고

너무나 작은 두 핑크

한 번은 멀리 한 번은 가까이
서로 만났다 헤어지고

연못에 빠진 작은 핑크는
하얀 공으로 살짝 바뀌고
숲속으로 날아간 핑크는 다시 또 핑크로 바뀌고

가끔은 쨍- 가끔은 퍽-
가끔은 신나게 가끔은 아쉽게
세상 밖으로 달려가고

A Pink Too Small

A pink too small

Furtively hiding in the green grass
Rolling gently slightly round and round

The two pinks too small

At one time at a distance and at another time nearby
They meet then part

The small pink that fell into the pond
Has transformed slightly into a white ball
The pink that flew into the forest has transformed again into pink

At times a clink— At times a pop—
At times cheerfully and at times regretfully
Running out into the world

모래에 빠진 핑크는
언제나 더 깊은 수렁에서 허우적대고

벼랑으로 떨어진 핑크는
오늘도 내일도 찾지 못하고

너무나 작은 핑크를 따라
이리저리 날아가는 핑크를 따라

오늘 하루도 왔다 갔다…

The pink that fell into the sand
Always floundering in a deeper pit

The pink that fell onto the cliff
Today and tomorrow is not to be found

Following a pink too small
Following a pink flying about here and there

Even today to and fro…

수박

차라리 아픈
차라리 잊혀질
속으로 속으로 감싸 안은 그리움은
더러는 검은 멍에를 남기고
더러는 초록의 담장을 치고
밀리어 떨어져 나가
대지의 숨소리를 고르고 있다

차라리 달콤한
차라리 신비로운
순수로 담아낸 빠알간 그리움은
더러는 상처를 남기고
더러는 풀 초롱 모습을 담아
밀리어 알알이 밝혀
자연의 향긋한 콧노래를 전하고 있다

Watermelon

Rather painful

Better to be forgotten

The yearning that embraces deep inside the heart

Sometimes leaves behind a black yoke

Sometimes kicks the green fence

Having dropped out from lagging behind

Makes the earth's sound even

Better as something sweet

Better as something mysterious

The red yearning that was filled with purity

Sometimes leaves a scar

Sometimes fills up with the image of a grass bell

Revealing everything from lagging behind

Delivers nature's fragrant humming

장미

소매 자락 마주 잡고
살갑게 포옹하며
고운 소리 발 맞추듯
싱그러운 그대 얼굴

소곤대는 그대 입술
닿을 듯 닿을 듯
사르르 입 맞추며
포르르 향기를 뿜어내는
달콤한 그대 입술

얼굴만 보아도 기쁘고
냄새만 맡아도 행복한

그대 이름은 장미

Rose

Taking hold of the cuffs

Embracing tenderly

Like keeping in pace with the gentle sounds

Your fresh face

Your whispering lips

Almost to touch almost to touch

Softly touching lips

Exuding an intoxicating scent

Your sweet lips

A joy just seeing your face

A bliss just smelling your scent

Your name is Rose

보랏빛 하늘에 담아

보랏빛 하늘에 담아
상큼한 과일을 하늘에 담아

두둥실 흘러가는 구름을 그리고
불어오는 열대 바람 소리를 새겨

하늘 속으로
구름 속으로
바람 속에서 햇살을 뚫고

기쁨을 모으고
슬픔을 밀어내는 열대 과일

크기도 다르지만
색깔도 다르지만

새콤한 향기를

Purple Light Filled in the Sky

Purple light filled in the sky
Fresh fruits filled in the sky

Drawing clouds lightly floating by
Seeping in the sound of the blowing tropical wind

Into the sky
Into the cloud
Having pierced through the sunshine in the wind

Gathering joy
Tropical fruits banishing sadness

Though different in size
Though different in color

The tart-zesty scent

달콤한 향기를

무지개로 나르는
보랏빛 하늘에 담아

우리네 시선을 모으고 있다

The sweet scent

Are placed in the purple sky
Flying as a rainbow

Attracting our gaze

치자 꽃

그리움을 감싸 안은 당신의 소매
흰나비 가냘픔을 배운 듯 하오

폭포의 순수로 접혀진 날개
승천하는 기쁨을 배운 듯 하오

안타깝게 깊어진 눈동자는
누구도 말없이 멈추게 하오

당신이 잉태한 한 아름 고독은
침묵의 절정을 배운 듯 하오

당신이 뿜어내는 찡-한 향기는
누구도 말없이 멈추게 하오

당신을 잃어버린 아픈 상처는
폭포의 전설도 멈추게 하오

A Gardenia Flower

Your sleeves embracing the longing
It's like you've learned the fragileness of a butterfly

Wings folded from the waterfall's purity
It's like you've learned how to ascend

Sadly your darkened eyes
Arrests anyone without a word

The armful solitude you've conceived
It's like you've learned the peak of silence

The potent scent you emit
Arrests anyone without a word

The painful scar that has forgotten you
Even makes the legend of the waterfall halt

눈

방울방울
반짝이는 은방울

날아와 앉는 또 날아와 앉는
신세계 교향곡의 만남과 헤어짐

동네를 돌아 산모퉁이를 돌아
반짝이며 흩어지는 차가운 보석
기쁨으로 새겨진 생명의 환희
사랑으로 아로새긴 탄생의 신비

살포시 내려앉은
예쁜 방석은

한 겨울의 따뜻한 은세계 교향곡

Snow

Snowflake by snowflake
Twinkling silver snowflake

Drifting in, again drifting in
The meeting and parting of the New World Symphony

Roving around the neighborhood, roving around the bend of
the mountain
The cold jewels twinkling and dispersing in all directions
The joy of life engraved with happiness
The mysteries of birth engraved with love

Softly drifting down
The pretty cushion

A warm Silver World Symphony of one winter

나이테

초록 바퀴는 연륜을 쌓고
끝없는 나이테를 물들여

진한 혈액 순환은
동맥과 정맥을 가르고

내 손만큼이나 어지러운 친구 생각은
오늘도 단단하게 여물어가고

바다 닮은 바퀴는 초록의 향기를 뿌리고 있다

거센 파도 장식도 마다하고
세찬 바람 소리도 마다하고

기쁨을 날줄삼아
슬픔을 씨줄삼아

Growth Rings

The green tire layered in years of experience
Stained with endless growth rings

The thick blood circulation
Split the arteries and veins

The dizzying thought of my friend as big as my hand
Today is also ripening firmly

The ocean-like tire sprays a green scent

Refusing even the decoration of the violent waves
Refusing even the sound of the fierce winds

Taking joy as longitude
Taking sadness as latitude

기다림 조각을 날리면서
적도로 적도로 향하고 있다

어느 날엔가

진노랑 붉음은 사라지고
뼈아픈 속도로 휘돌면서
나이를 잊고 사는
우리들 나팔소리는 점점 커진다

Throwing away pieces of a thousand months
Heading towards the equator the equator

One of these days

The mustard redness will disappear
Spinning at a painful speed
Nonchalant towards age
The sound of our trumpet grows louder and louder

봄 눈

겨울이 아쉬워
봄이 그리워

하얗게 흔드는 차가운 손수건

먼 나라 동화 속
하얀 궁전에
잠자는 백설공주
차가운 행복을 부르고

하얀 외투로 갈아입은 소나무
따사로운 우리 엄마 품속

사뿐히 내려앉은 봄 눈

겨울이 아쉬워
새 봄이 그리워

Spring Snow

Winter is being missed
Spring is being longed for

The cold handkerchief waving in white

In a faraway land of a children's tale
At a white palace
Sleeping Snow White
Calling out a cold bliss

A pine tree changed into a white coat
The warm bosom of my mom

The spring snow falling lightly

Winter is being missed
Spring is being longed for

하얗게 하얗게
내려앉으며

내가 사온
수채화 물감처럼
멀리 저 멀리 흩날리고 있다.

In white in white

Drifting down

They flutter about far far away

Like the watercolors

I have bought.

눈 오리

눈이 좋아 눈 장난 좋아하네
눈사람 만들던 민이
눈싸움 잘하던 진이
눈을 닮은 하얀 친구라네

오늘은 눈이 오네
민이 생각 진이 생각
내 마음 눈 날개 달았네
하얀 눈 날개 달았네
높이 더 높이 날아보네

눈이 좋아 눈사람 만들었네
친구 없어 눈싸움 할 수 없네

까만 털실 수놓은 하얀 친구
오늘은 하얀 눈 오리 되었네

Snow Duck

Fond of snow like playing with snow
Minnie who had made snowmen
Jinnie who had been good at snowball fighting
A white friend like snow

Snow is falling today
Thoughts of Minnie thoughts of Jinnie
My heart has been hoisted with snow wings
Hoisted with white snow wings
Flying high and higher

Fond of snow I have made a snowman
Without a friend no snowball fight for me

A white friend embroidered with black wool
Has become a white snow duck

폭설

오랜만에 내리는 폭설

천년 바위를 흔들어 깨우는
신선한 충격

먼 나라 동화 속
잠들고픈 숲 속에
끝없이 펼쳐 놓은 고요한 잠자리

새벽 아내 조바심되어
부지런한 엄마 품속에서
힘차게 힘차게 달리는 적막

Heavy Snowfall

A heavy snowfall not seen in a while

A fresh shock
That shakes and wakes up the 1,000-year boulder

In a faraway land of a children's tale
Inside the sleepy forest
The tranquil bed stretching endlessly

The early-bird wife gone anxious
In the bosom of a hard-working mom
The silence racing vigorously vigorously

조개

너는 모래성의 귀빈

온종일 파도의 대접을 받고
바다의 보석을 입 안 가득

너는 모래성의 비밀

파도가 칠한 고운 색깔로
멋진 성 짓고

너는 모래성의 파수

두꺼운 갑옷으로 몸치장하고
고뇌의 총구멍만 빠끔

너는 모래성의 영웅

Clam

You are the sandcastle's distinguished guest

Receiving special treatment from the ocean all day
Your mouth full of the ocean's gems

You are the sandcastle's secret

With the pretty colors painted by the waves
You build beautiful castles

You are the sandcastle's guard

Clad in heavy armor
With the entire pores of anguish only split apart

You are the sandcastle's hero

고독한 영혼 속에 쌓인 비밀을
온몸 가득

너를 닮고파 네가 보고파
길을 떠난다
파도 소리 춤추는 바다로

The secret filled up in your lonely soul

Consumes your whole body

Wanting to be like you I miss you

I'm leaving the passage

For the ocean where the sound of the waves dance

등대

침묵의 검은 피로 멍들어
끝없는 청춘을 부수고 있소

세찬 음향에 귀가 멀고
푸른 야망에 눈빛은 바래

의미 잃은 한 눈만 껌벅이며
울부짖는 바다를 달래고 있소

웅크러진 사랑의 접힘인가?

슬픔의 핏방울만 떨어뜨리며
파도에 일렁이는 작은 종이배

당신의 몸뚱이에 생명 걸었소
암갈색 몸뚱이에 생명 걸었소

Lighthouse

Bruised by the dark blood of silence
You are destroying the eternal youth

Deafened by strong sounds
The twinkle in your eyes faded by blue ambitions

Only one eye that has lost meaning blinks
You calm the howling ocean

Could it be the ripples of a crumpled love?

Only dripping blood drops of sadness

A small paper boat rocking on the waves

You have staked your life on your body
You have staked your life on your dark-brown body

번민은 끓어버린 거품에 녹고
진통을 잉태한 당신은
대화 잃은 암갈색 몸뚱이로
고뇌의 검은 멍만 키우고 있소

어제도 오늘도 잃어버리고

Your suffering has melted in the bubbling froth

Pregnant with contractions

With your dark-brown body that has lost all conversation

You are only growing a black bruise of anguish

Forgetting yesterday and today

제3부 Section 3

시간과 공간을 넘어 *Beyond Time and Space*

밤

경쾌한 초저녁 지나
어둡고 창백한 밤

몇 개의 조각을 늘어놓고 또 이어놓는 내 작업
미완성 그림을 그리는 화가처럼
조약돌로 그려진 차창처럼
하얀 선율만 남겨놓는 시각

행여 기적을 바라는 마음은
천 길 아래 흘러버린 용암처럼
어둠과 고열의 증기만 뿜어내고

돌아와 누운 참숯덩이는
기쁨 위한 점화를 배우건만
슬픔과 아픔만 새겨지고

빛을 향해 달려가는 또 하나의 시각 – 밤

Night

Past the cheerful early hours of the evening
The dark and lifeless night

My job to spread out the pieces continuously
Like a painter working on an unfinished piece
Like a car window outlined with pebbles
A perspective where only the white melody is left

The feeling of having to wait for a miracle
Like lava that has flowed under the stream
Spewing out only darkness and super-hot steam

The lump of hardwood charcoal lying down upon its return
Only having learned the spark for happiness
Engraved with only sadness and pain

Another perspective of running towards the light – night

어느 날

어느 이른 아침
어느 초저녁

휘감고 퍼지는 하얀 미소가
하얗게 바래버린 연민을

어느 노을 속에서
환상의 햇살을 삼키고

철길 따라 뻗어가는 순수를 찾아
그저 달리는 그리움을

늘어 늘어 높이 선 남산 길 돌계단을
하나, 둘, 다섯

널려 널려 잘 익은 노란 자두를
하나, 둘, 다섯

One Day

One early morning
One early evening

The white smile coiling and spreading
The pity that has faded into white

Inside a sunset
Swallowing the illusion of sunlight

Finding the expanding purity following the railroad track
Nothing but the racing longing

On the rising rising high-standing stone stairway of Mt. Namsan road
One, two, five

The scattered scattered well-ripened yellow plums
One, two, five

그저 오르고

그저 깨물며

아이는 상큼한 눈웃음을

Just climbing

Just biting

The child with refreshing smiling eyes

생일

떨어진 낙엽 위를 걷는다
차가운 침묵이 흐른다

교회의 종소리가 들리고
취객의 고함 소리가 높아진다

사치스런 촛불과 꽃다발은
환상처럼 조각조각 흩날리고

바람 소리 가득한 종이배는
파도 소리 담으며 팔랑인다

Birthday

I walk over the fallen leaves
A cold silence resonates

I hear the church bells ringing
The drunken man's shout grows louder

The extravagant candlelight and bouquet
Flutter like an illusion in pieces

The paper boat full of the sound of the wind
Floats as it loads the sound of the waves

보름

우리는 떠나고 있다
환상의 고향에서 몸부림치고
슬픔과 고통을 잊으려고
내일을 향해 달리고 있다

돌아보고 있다
회전하는 얼음판 팽이처럼
힘차게 돌아가는 할머니 맷돌처럼

계속 따라오는 보름달
우리보다 더 큰 부끄러움
앞뒤로 따라오는 수줍은 달

축배를 든 투명한 거품 속으로
우리는 떠나고 있다
황량한 산등어리를 지나
힘겨운 모순을 끌어안고
대보름을 향해 그믐을 향해 달리고 있다

Day of the Full Moon

We are departing

Struggling in our illusionary hometown

Trying to forget the sadness and agony

We are racing towards tomorrow

Looking back

Like a rotating icy top

Like grandmother's powerfully rotating millstone

The full moon following us continuously

More bashful than us

A bashful moon that follows us from back and front

Into the transparent bubbles of the beholden drink toast

We are leaving

Past the bleak mountain ridge

Embracing the arduous contradiction

Racing towards the full moon towards the end of the month

함지박에 누워

함지박에 누워
바다 향한 꿈을 키우고
넓은 유리벽 넘어
바다 저편 돛단배 자유를 배운다

정동진 예술은 하늘과 바다의 만남
너와 나의 만남은 하늘과 바다가 빚은 예술

어린 소나무의 애틋한 사연과
뚱뚱한 아줌마의 풍요로운 기쁨은
하늘을 향해 바다를 향해
두 손을 번쩍 들고

맛깔스런 전복죽 감칠맛은
동해 바다 향이 가득하고
쫄깃한 감자송편 깔끔함은
강원도 아낙네 손맛이 가득하고
조개 굽는 따닥 타다닥 소리는

Lying on the Large Wooden Bowl

Lying on the large wooden bowl
Nurturing a dream towards the ocean
Over the wide glass wall
Learning the freedom of the sailboat across the sea

The art of settling east is the meeting of the sky and the ocean
The meeting of you and me is the art created by the sky and the ocean

The fond story of the young pine tree
The bountiful joy of a fat lady
Toward the sky toward the ocean
With both hands straight up

The tastiness of the perfect abalone porridge
Brims with the scent of the east sea
The cleanliness of chewy potato rice cakes
Oozes the home cooking of a Gangwon-do woman
The crackling sound of roasting clams

서로의 가슴을 꿰뚫어보고

푹—퍽 푹—퍽 다가오는 기차 소리는
우리 머리를 지나
연보라 저녁노을 속으로 달려가고

젊은이 등에 진 배낭은
우리 눈 속에서 춤을 추고
함께 잡은 두 손에는
어느새 살가운 바람 소리가 휘이이

함지박에 누운
우리네 만남은

하얀 이를 드러내는 돛단배 되어 까르르르르

Pierces through each of our hearts

Clackety-clack, clackety-clack the sound of a train drawing near
Passes our heads
And races into the violet sunset glow

The backpack on a young person's back
Dances in our eyes
In our two clasped hands
The tender sound of the wind howls before we know it

Our meeting
Laid on a large a wooden bowl

Becomes a sailboat that screeches exposing our white teeth

꿈을 꾸면서

꿈을 꾸면서
별들이 째근대는 하늘을 보며 누워 있다
습관처럼
별들의 숨소리를 듣는다

즐거운 예감이다
아낌없이 주는 나무를 만나는 꿈
코주부 아저씨가 내미는 과자
꿈으로 가득 채운 밤하늘
좋은 꿈이겠지

파도 소리 들으며
바다 향기 맡으며
서로를 향하여 부르는
밤하늘의 노랫소리
꿈을 꾸면서
별을 보면서
복이 가득한 네 귀를 잡는다

As I Dream

As I dream
I am lying down looking at the sky permeated with the breath of stars
Like a habit
I listen to the breathing of the stars

It's a joyful feeling
A dream where I meet a tree that gives generously
A cookie offered by a big-nosed man
The night sky filled with dreams
It should be a good dream

Listening to the sound of the waves
Smelling the fragrant of the ocean
Singing towards each other
The songs of the night sky
As I dream
As I look at the stars
I hold your ear full of blessings

이삭 줍게 하소서

찬란한 향연이 열렸던 이 곳
하얗게 휘몰아친 당신의 명命에
껍데기만 남겨 둔 농부의 바램

까마득한 옛날의 꿈속에서
소스라쳐 깨어나는 두 눈에는
달래줄 손길만 부르짖을 뿐
황금색 익은 꿈은 잊은 지 오래

대지여!
허락하소서
당신이 살찌운 넓은 공간에
풍성한 마음을 두게 하소서

당신의 알뜰한 사랑의 잔상
먼 훗날 향연에 바치오리다
곱고 착한 등허리에 가득 실어서

Let Us Gather Grains

This place once occupied with a glorious feast

Your orders that swept through clean

The farmer's hopes for just remnants of the shell

In the dream of the distant past

In the two eyes awakened by a startle

Only the soothing hands clamoring

Been long since the golden-ripe dream has been forgotten

Mother Earth!

Permit us

In the swollen vast space you have provided

Allow us to have a bountiful heart

The remnants of your frugal love

Will be offered to you through a feast in the distant future

Abundantly carried on my lovely and kind back

귀향

환하게 피어난 연꽃 사이로
구멍구멍 파이던 어느 스산한 귀향 길

등 뒤를 매섭게 후려치는 옛날이야기는
어느덧 무지개를 삼켜버리고

노을로 태어난 전설은
어느새 산 저편에 숨고
부끄러운 보름달은 중천에 걸려

누구도 기다리지 않는 발길을 알아차린

까만 소리를 내는 밤

언젠가 잃어버린 파안의 미소는
맥 빠진 하늘을 곱게 그리고

The Homecoming

Between the radiantly bloomed lotus flower
The dreary road to returning home with potholes

The old story that harshly beats the back
Had before we realized swallowed up the rainbow

The legend born as the sunset
Before we knew it had hid far beyond the mountain
The bashful moonlight caught high up in the sky

Realization of the footsteps no one waits for

The night making a black sound

The smile lost at some point
Gently draws the disheartened sky

팔딱이며 달려가는 산허리는
찬바람에 오싹하는 은행잎처럼
스스로 접혀진 나의 몸짓에

귀향의 기쁨을
쏟아내는 여름은
어느새 낙엽 되어
바삭바삭 겨울을 열고 있는

까맣게 익어가는 밤

The hillside racing with leaps

Like a ginkgo tree leaf shivering in the cold wind

On my gestures I have folded away

The summer pouring out

The joy of returning home

Has all too soon turned into dead leaves

Cracking open winter

Is the night ripening into black

산 속에서

산 속에서 보내는 한적한 오후
나무 향기 풀 향기
꽃 향기 가득한 산 속에서

삐르륵 또록 컥컥 또로록 쫑쫑
또르르르 뻐뻐꾹 뻐꾹

산새들 노랫소리를 듣는다

휘이이 지나가는 바람 소리에
돌돌돌 흘러가는 물소리에

계곡을 따라
내 귓가를 넘어오는
자연의 교향곡을 듣는다

친구가 지어낸 우스갯소리에

In the Mountains

A quiet afternoon in the mountains
Tree scent grass scent
In the mountains filled with the scent of flowers

Chirrup cheep chirp chirrup chirp
Chirrup cheep chirp

Listening to the singing of the mountain birds

In the sound of the wind whishing by
In the sound of the water trickling down

Following the valley
I listen to Nature's Symphony
Crossing over to the rim of my ear

At the joke made by my friend

손뼉을 치며 무릎을 치며
작은 가슴으로 큰 산을 울리며

하하하 큰 소리로
까르르르 작은 소리로
또 하나의 협주곡을 연주하며

오늘도 나는 산 속에서
산을 닮은 싱그러움을 배우고 있다

I clap my hands slap my knees

A small heart making a big mountain reverberate

With a loud ha ha ha

With a quiet burst of a snort

Performing another symphony

Another one of my days in the mountains

I am learning the freshness like that of the mountains

백봉령 고갯마루

산모퉁이를 지나 푸른 솔밭을 지나
백봉령 고갯마루에
사뿐히 내려앉은 뭉게구름

오두막 주막 뜰엔
주인 아낙네의 손빨래가
상쾌한 산바람을 맞는 오후

산등성이를 따라
산기슭을 따라
숨 가쁘게 노래하는 산새 소리

메밀부침 속 실파는 어느덧
친구의 마음을 빼앗고

친구와 마주 앉은 낙락장송 진한 향기는
행복한 웃음소리가 되고

The Top of Baekbongryeong

Past the spur of a mountain past the green pine grove
On the top of Baekbongryeong
Fluffy clouds land lightly

In the yard of the cabin inn
The hand laundry of the inn owner's wife
An afternoon with the greeting of the fresh mountain breeze

Along the ridge of the mountain
Along the foot of the mountain
The sound of a mountain bird singing breathlessly

At some moment the green onions in the pan-fried buckwheat dough
Had stolen my friend's heart

The strong scent of the tall and exuberant pine tree facing my
friend and me

하늘로 뻗어 오른 산마루에는
옛날 장터를 꿈꾸는 추억이 두런두런

뻑뻐꾹 뻐국 소리에
깊은 산 오후는 저물고
동동주에 취한 내 친구는
쉬어가는 졸음에 낮잠 청한다

오두막 지나는 산바람 소리에
하루가 지나가는 백봉령 고갯마루에
아쉬운 몸짓을 남기고
우리는 자꾸만 돌아본다

Becomes the sound of a happy laughter

On the mountain ridge reaching up to the sky
Memories of dreaming about the old marketplace linger

In the sounds of creaks and squeaks
The late afternoon in the mountains nears a close
My friend drunk on *dongdongju**
Requests a nap in drowsiness

In the sound of the mountain breeze passing by the cabin
In the day passing by at the top of Baekbongryeong
We sadly leave behind our gestures
And we keep looking back

Dongdongju is Korean rice wine.

신흥사 앞뜰

고즈넉한 산사 옆에
나지막한 오두막

기름이 자르르
부추향이 가득한 감자전

천사 닮은 아주머니
비단 같은 미소로 나를 반기고

돌돌돌 흘러가는 물소리
끼르륵 또르르 날아가는 새소리
산사에서 들려오는 목탁소리
행복한 친구 웃음소리
나를 깨우는 상큼한 아침 산책

신흥사 앞뜰에 앉아
기쁜 함성을 듣는 행복한 아침

The Front Yard of Sinheungsa Temple

Beside the quiet and peaceful mountain temple
The low-standing hut

The pan-fried potato dough filled with the aroma of leek
Glossy with grease

An angel-like middle-aged woman
Greets me with a silk-like smile

The trickling sound of flowing water
The flapping fluttering sound of the flying bird
The sound of the wooden gong from the mountain temple
The laughter of a happy friend
The fresh morning stroll that awakens me

Sitting in the front yard of Sinheungsa Temple
Is a pleasant morning resounding with joyful cheering

바다

광활한 가슴으로 푸르름 다해
힘차게 뿌리고 부서지는 영혼을 보듯
침묵의 나를 향한 몸짓

언어의 가난함은 떠나보내고
가난한 가슴만 품어버린
수평선 저쪽의 긴 그림자

물망초 설움 익은 잎이 되고자

벼랑을 기어내린 촛농의 진실은
지우고픈 기억으로 샘을 파고

보랏빛 시선 머문 당신 얼굴엔
구름 그린 하늘 그림자가 너울댄다

The Ocean

Committed to blueness with its vast heart

Powerfully scattering and like seeing the shattering soul

Its gestures directed at silent me

Letting go the poverty of language

Dismissing only the poor soul

The long shadow of the distant horizon

Becoming a forget-me-not leaf ripe with sorrow

The candle dripping's truth that has climbed down the cliff

Burrows through the spring with memories that want to be forgotten

On your face fixed with a violet gaze

Are the swelling shadows of the sky with drawings of clouds

화진포 여행

바닷길 따라
춤을 추는 안개 속에서

친구 얼굴이 보이고
하늘이 보이고
바다가 보이고
환하게 웃는 화진포 아이가
안개길 따라 모래 위를 달리고

키 작은 소나무 따뜻한 눈빛이
안개가 휘돌아간 바다를 따라

길지 않은 역사와 세월을 따라
기쁨과 행복으로 가득차고

차르르 사르르 밀려가는 파도 소리에
하얗게 부서지는 파도 소리에

Trip to Hwajinpo

Along the seawall
In the frolicking fog

I see my friend's face
I see the sky
I see the ocean
The brightly smiling Hwajinpo child
Along the foggy pathway I run through the sand

The warm gaze of a small pine tree
Along the ocean where the fog had come and gone

The short history and passing of time
Filled with joy and happiness

Swish swash in the sound of the rolling waves
In the sound of the waves shattering to white

어제와 오늘이 지워지고

끼르륵 끄르륵 날아가는 바닷새소리에
슬픔과 아픔이 스러지고

바다 저만치 뻗어나간 수평선 따라
내일 향한 작은 꿈 익어가고

힘차게 솟아오른 산기슭 따라
쩌렁쩌렁 울리는 친구 목소리
내 가슴 내 마음 울리고

친구 닮은 안개 속 바다는
은빛 바다 향기로 다가선다

Yesterday and tomorrow washed away

Swoosh swoosh in the sound of the soaring sea birds
Sadness and pain disappear

Along the horizon spanning as widely as the ocean
Tomorrow's small dream ripens

Along the foot of the mountain powerfully soaring upwards
The loud resonating voice of my friend
Reverberates through my heart and my emotions

The ocean in the fog resembling my friend
Draws close to the fragrant of the silver ocean

정선읍 돌아

더덕 향 가득한 정선읍에서
메밀전병을 먹고
곤드래 밥을 먹고

둘이 또 함께
내 고향소리를 듣고
네 고향소리를 듣고

시장모퉁이를 돌아
내 행복을 사고 네 기쁨을 사고

두 손 가득한 봉지는
사각사각 부딪는 소리를 내고
처마 밑 제비는
삐륵 삐륵 아기새 먹이를 나르고
눈빛 마주친 아주머니는
인정 넘치는 인사를 하고

Trip Around Jeongseon-eup

At Jeongseon-eup filled with the scent of deodeok herb root
Eating buckwheat pancakes
Ravenously eating rice

The two of us together
I hear the sounds of my hometown
I hear the sounds of your hometown

Turning the corner of the market
I buy my happiness and buy your joy

My two hands full of bags
Hit each other making crackling sounds
The swallow under the eaves
Flies food over to the baby swallows
Upon eye contact with the middle-aged woman
I am given a warm greeting

정선읍 풍경에 취한 친구는
굽이굽이 돌아가는 정선 길을
아리아리 돌아가는 아리랑을
휘파람 소리로 화답 하고

우리는 또 함께
산 길 따라 강 길 따라 바다로 가고
보라색 구름 속 동해로 가고
밀려오는 파도 소리 처얼썩 처르르

친구의 속삭임 소곤소곤
아름답고 시원한 화음 따라
신나게 뻗어나간 기찻길 따라
정선읍 돌아가는 하루를 닫으려 한다

My friend intoxicated from Jeongseong-eup's landscape

The meandering curvy roads of Jeongseon

The Ari Ari roundabout way of Arirang

Are answered with the sounds of whistling

We are again together

We go to the sea following the mountain road, the riverside road

We go to the East Sea into the purple clouds

The flushing sound of the waves rushing in

The whisperings of my friend

Following the beautiful and refreshing sound of harmony

Joyfully following the sprawling railroad tracks

I seek to bring to a close the day at Jeongseong-eup

눈 덮인 여름 산

꼬마 기차를 타고
눈 덮인 여름 산 너머
얼음이 떠나간 길목에서

배를 타고 건너가는 그 옛날

눈 덮인 여름 산에서
그 옛날 저 멀리서

아름답게 지나가는 여인네 노랫소리

하얀 눈 빨간 옷
너무나 아름다운

눈 덮인 여름 산
싸늘한 추억

The Snow-Covered Summer Mountain

Riding on a mini train

Over the snow-covered summer mountain

At the corner of the road with broken ice

Those old days when boats carried us across

In the snow-covered summer mountain

Those old days from afar

The lady's singing beautifully flowing by

White snow red clothes

So beautiful

The snow-covered summer mountain

A cold memory

억년을 지켜온 빙하
세상을 떠나가는 인사를 하고

숨 가쁘게 펄떡이는 연어는
나그네 기쁨으로 태어나고

기차를 타고
또다시 꼬마기차를 타고
눈 덮인 여름 산 넘어

손발이 꽁꽁 어는 겨울 여행을 한다

The glacier that has observed millions of years

Has greeted the passing of time

The salmon whose breath joyously trembles

Has been born with the joys of a traveler

Riding a train

And again riding the mini train

Over the snow-covered summer mountain

I am on a winter's journey that freezes my hands and toes

달려가는 모래 언덕

앞이 보이지 않는
모래 언덕
한참을 달려도 끝이 없는
모래만 가득한 사막

파삭한 모래 바람 속으로
부서져 내리는 우리네 삶

올라갔다 거꾸러지고
숨 가쁘게 내려갔다 올라가는
어느 사막 모래 언덕

박수소리가 들리고
비명소리가 들리고
아이들 웃음소리가 들리는
우리네 삶처럼

The Racing Sand Dune

Nothing in sight
The sand dune
The end not in sight despite the traveled distance
A desert only full of sand

Into the wind with dusty sand
Our existence crumbling down

Tumbling on the climb up
Breathing hard
A sand dune in some desert

The sound of clapping resonates
The sound of screaming resonates
The sound of children's laughter audible
Like our everyday life

모래 벼랑 끝에서
숨을 죽이며
미끄러졌다 다시 솟구치면서
앞사람 뒷사람 부여잡으며
끝없이 달려가는 모래 언덕

바람 속에 흩어지는
모래 언덕 너머로
긴 낙타 여행이 보이고
수렁으로 빠져드는 모래 속에서
작은 개미 여행이 보이고

우리네 삶처럼
멀리 저 멀리서 노을이 진다

On the edge of the sand cliff

Suppressing my breath

I slip then pick myself up again

Clutching onto the person in front and behind

Endlessly racing along the sand dune

Dispersing in the wind

Over the sand dune

I see a long camel journey

Sinking into a pit in the sand

I see a small ant journey

Like our everyday life

The sun sets in the distance far away

프라하의 아침

흑백이 어우러진 검은 도시 속에서

도시를 가르는 강을 만나고
옛사랑 이어주는 다리를 건너

카프카의 멋진 얼굴도 읽어보고
옛 장인의 시계 소리도 들어보고

도시가 연주 하는 협주곡을 듣는 아침

어제 가본 그 옛날 오페라 극장도 생각나고
그제 가본 높은 언덕 위 카프카 무덤도 생각나고

흑백 도시에서

고대와 현대를 만나고
중세 음악을 들으면서

The Morning in Prague

In the black city with black and white in harmony

I meet the river passing through the city
Crossing over the bridge that liaises with a bygone love

Have read into the handsome face of Kafka
Have heard the sound of the master-crafted ancient clock

A morning where the symphony performed by the city resonates

The age-old opera theatre visited yesterday comes to mind
Kafka's grave on the high hill visited the day before yesterday also
comes to mind

In the black-and-white city

I meet the ancient and the modern times

프라하 맥주를 마시는

동서양 친구들 노랫소리가 깨어나는 아침

아침 미사를 알리는 청아한 종소리가
우리를 깨우고

검은 도시로 달리는 아침 햇살은
프라하 아침교향곡을 연주한다

Listening to music of the middle ages

A morning waken up by the singing of Eastern and Western friends
Who drink the beer of Prague

The clear bell sound signaling time for morning mass
Wakes us up

The morning sun racing towards the black city
Performs the Prague Morning Symphony

펭귄 고향을 찾아

아주 작은 산을 만나고
끝없이 펼쳐진 산을 보면서
정말로 예쁜 산 무덤 따라
펭귄 고향을 찾아
남으로 바다로 내려간다

검은 바위에 걸터앉아
조용조용 소곤소곤 속삭이며
펭귄 고향을 찾아
밤으로 하늘로 올라간다

저 멀리서
바다 저편 저 멀리서
나를 향해 걸어오는
뒤뚱뒤뚱 걸어오는 펭귄 또 펭귄
밤안개 속에서
물안개 속에서

Heading to the Home of Penguins

Upon meeting a very small mountain
Looking at the endless stretch of mountains
Along the sublimely beautiful mountain tomb
Heading to the home of penguins
I travel north to the ocean

Perched on a black rock
Whispering quietly
Heading to the home of penguins
I ascend into the night, the sky

From a far distance
Across the ocean from a far distance
Walking towards me
A penguin waddling forth then another penguin
In the night fog
In the wet fog

보였다 안 보이는 아주 작은 몸짓
아주 많은 몸짓

우리는 숨죽이며
큰 눈을 더 크게 뜨고
너무나 작은 발자국 소리를
너무나 귀여운 펭귄을 기다리고 있다

친구인지 가족인지
나란히 나란히 내 앞을 지나
작은 다리 밑으로

작은 오솔길 지나
예쁜 산 무덤 속으로
하나 또 하나 들어간다

작은 날개로 사랑 나누며

Visible then non-visible the very small gestures

The very big gestures

Holding our breath

Opening our big eyes even wider

The very faintly sounding footsteps

Waiting for the very cute penguins

Whether friend or family

They pass by me in a line

Under a small bridge

Past the narrow path

Into the pretty mountain tomb

They enter one by one

Sharing love with their small wings

작은 몸짓으로 인사를 하며
산 무덤 속으로
하나 또 하나 잠을 청한다

너무나 작고 너무나 귀여운
펭귄 고향을 찾아
작은 목소리를 들으며
작은 몸짓을 배우며
차가운 밤하늘을 나누고 있다

온몸을 떨면서
아주 작은 펭귄을 가슴에 담고
새벽 향해 달리는
버스를 탄다

이제 산 무덤은 보이지 않고
꿈속을 헤매는 잠꼬대만
여기저기서 쌔근쌔근 잠잠

Greeting with small motions

Into the tiny mountain tomb

They try to sleep one by one

Heading to the home of penguins

So small and so cute

Listening to the small voices

Learning the small gestures

I share the cold night sky

With my whole body shaking

I carry the very small penguin in my heart

And get on the bus

That is racing towards morning

With the tiny mountain tomb no longer in sight

Wandering about in a dream I talk in my sleep

Peaceful and serene here and there

화산섬 하루

1

싱그러운 마음이 이곳에 모여
향그러운 사랑이 이곳에 모여

꽃을 피우고 꽃 섬을 만들고

은빛 마음이 어우러져
금빛 사랑이 뒤엉켜서

바다를 만들고 하늘을 만들고

타오르는 사랑이
뜨거운 열정이

깊고 깊은 곳에
커다란 불꽃을 끌어안고

A Day on a Volcanic Island

1

Fresh feelings gather at this place
Fragrant love gathers at this place

Make flowers bloom and make a flower island

With a silver heart in harmony
With a golden love entangled

Making the ocean and making the sky

The raging love
The hot passion

At the deep and profound site
Embracing the large flame

타오르는 불씨는 여기에서
타오르는 사랑은 저기에서
어지러운 유황냄새를 뿜으며

희뿌연 재를 남기며

화산섬 하루가 지나간다

2
파도 소리에 잠이 들고
바다 향기에 잠이 깨고

얼굴을 스쳐가는 바람 소리에
귓전을 울리는 새소리에

또 하루가 지난다

The raging embers here
The raging love there
Emitting the dizzying smell of sulfur

Leaving hazy ashes

A day at the volcanic island passes

2

Falling asleep with the sound of the waves
Awakening from the smell of the ocean

In the sound of the wind caressing the face
In the roaring sound of the birds

Another day passes by

3

눈 덮인 화산이 나를 부르고
타오르는 화산이 나를 부르고

무지개 구름을 따라
천둥과 번개를 치며
옥빛 바다를 건너
먹빛 용암을 따라

오늘 하루도 간다

3

The snow-covered volcano calls out to me

The raging volcano calls out to me

Along with the rainbow cloud

Thunder and lightning striking

Across the jade-colored ocean

Following the ink-black lava

Today also is passing by

마카오 여행

1

날개를 단 쾌속정

바다인지 강인지
크기를 보면 바다
색깔을 보면 강
서해 바다를 닮은 것인지
서해 바다가 닮은 것인지
의혹은 호기심을 낳고
호기심은 긴장으로 변한다

2

길가에 늘어선 상점
창가에 널어놓은 어지러운 빨래

첫 골목은 20년을 더듬고
호떡가게가 보이고

Trip to Macao

1

A speedboat with wings

Whether an ocean or a river
In size like an ocean
In color like a river
Whether it resembles the west coast
Whether the west coast resembles it
Suspicion gives birth to curiosity
Curiosity transforms to tension

2

Shops lined up along the street
Laundry erratically hanging out the window

The first alley traces back 20 years
Can see a Chinese pancake shop

만두가게가 보이고
강아지와 병아리 말다툼이 들린다

두 번째 골목은 10년을 뒤집고
굽이굽이 돌아가는 작은 오솔길
나지막하게 줄지어 늘어선 집

하루는 20년을 넘어
도시는 꿈속을 넘나든다

　　3
400년 그림자를 짊어지고
외따로 지켜온 그 옛날 영토
마르코 폴로 넋 지킨
무너지지 않은 또 다른 성벽

두들겨도 깨지지 않는 종이창 신비

Can see a dumpling shop

Can hear the squabbling of a puppy and a chick

The second alley turns over 10 years

A small meandering curvy trail

A house lined up in a low row of homes

One day leaping past 20 years

The city crosses over into a dream

3

Carrying a 400-year-old shadow

That ancient territory guarded alone

That has protected Marco Polo's spirit

Another indomitable castle wall

The mysteriousness of the paper window that doesn't shatter even
when knocked at

4

스님의 정성 담긴 생명의 나무
구불구불 구부러져 목숨 수(壽) 만들었네
마카오 운명 위한 목숨인가
아니면 그 옛날 인간의 욕망?

지금은 소망되어 더욱 푸르고
오가는 우리네 희망 되어
자기 껍데기가 벗겨져도
자기 몸매가 구부러져도
언제나 푸르른 부모인 양
정겹고 성실한 생명의 나무

5

아주 예쁜 종이 상자
종이 사람이 보이고
종이 옷이 보이고

4

The tree of life with a monk's heartfelt devotion

Has created a winding bent life

Is it for the fate of Macao?

Or is it the desires of the people of the past?

Now hoped for it is even greener

Becoming our hope, of those coming and going

Even if its shell comes off

Even if its figure bends

Always the volume of one's greenish parents

The affectionate and faithful tree of life

5

A very pretty paper box

Can see a paper person

Can see paper clothes

종이 신발이 보인다

촛불과 향불 속으로
점점 아득하게 타버린다
우리가 가득 채운 종이 상자가
친구가 보내준 종이 돈이
동짓달 연기 속에서 희뿌연 재를 남기며
팔랑팔랑 바람을 부비며 날아가고 있다

    6
빈 기둥만 남아
구멍 뚫린 기둥만 남아
안과 밖이 통하고
위와 아래가 통하고
동서가 만나고 남북이 갈라져
수백 계단을 오르고서도
아득한 성모상

Can see paper shoes

Into the candlelight and incense
Gradually burning away into the distance
The paper box we had filled up
The paper money sent by a friend
Leaving hazy ashes in the smoke of the 11th month of the lunar calendar
Flying away fluttering against the wind

6

Left with only empty pillars
Left with only perforated pillars
With the inside and outside in flow
With the top and bottom in flow
The East-West meet and the South-North divide
Even having climbed hundreds of stairs
The far-off statue of the Virgin Mary

웅장함으로 버티어
우뚝 서 지키는 옛 성벽

그러나 지금은 빈 껍데기
정말로 지금은 빈 껍데기
속 빠져 구멍 뚫린 빈 껍데기

7

담배연기 속으로 몇 백 년이 묻히고
연기 속에서 잃어버린 동행자를 찾는다
6각형인지 8각형인지
구분할 수 없는 판들
아래도 가득 위에도 가득
이쪽도 가득 저쪽도 가득

기계 소리 동전 소리
다시 쏟아지는 소리 속으로

Enduring on grandiosity

The ancient castle wall standing high in guard

But now an empty shell

Truly now an empty shell

A hollow perforated empty shell

   7

Hundreds of years buried into cigarette smoke

Looking for a companion lost in the smoke

Whether a hexagon or an octagon

Panels difficult to separate

Full at the bottom and full at the top

Full on this side and full on that side

The sound of machines and the sound of coins

Into the sound pouring out once again

하나를 먹고 둘을 먹고
어쩌다 들어맞은 행운은
부처님 자비로 돌리고
동행자는 까르르…
악수와 함성은 귓전을 울린다

8

시원한 눈매
손가락 잘린 장갑
상냥한 미소와 재치 있는 설명
날개 편 뱃전에 몸을 싣는다
색색의 여권만 보아도
마카오는 국제도시
그래도 마주 보고 서로 웃는
우리는 친구
마카오 하루를 함께 보냈다

Consuming one and consuming two

The luck that strikes on the rare occasion

Is ascribed to the mercy of Buddha

My companion bursts into laughter⋯

The handshakes and shouts ring the rim of the ear

8

The bright eyes

The fingerless gloves

The friendly smile and witty explanations

Washing the body from the winged side of the boat

Just looking at the colorful passport

Macao is a cosmopolitan city

Still facing each other smiling

We are friends

We spent our day in Macao together

세상을 이야기하는 '소리'의 세계

윤 여 탁

(문학평론가 · 서울대 교수)

1

내게 글쓰기의 선택권이 주어진다면 피하려는 일 중에 하나가 잘 아는 사람의 작품에 대한 글쓰기이다. 그런데 어느 날 나는 시집 출간에 대해서 궁금해하는 메일과 전화를 신현숙 시인에게서 받았다. 그 질문에 대해서 개인 시집 출간이 어려운 일이 아니며, 시인이 되는 여러 방법 중 하나가 시집 출간이라고 답장을 보냈다. 그 후 며칠 사이에 시집 출간에 필요한 몇 가지 조언과 안내가 오고 갔고, 오래 지나지 않아 조판된 시집이 나에게 배달되었다. 이런 일련의 일들이 아주 신속하게 진행되었다. 이 과정에서 나는 새로운 시인의 탄생을 축하했고, 간행되는 시집에 대한 해설도 써달라는 부탁도 받았다. 마치 꿈을 꾸는 것과 같은 이 이야기는 사실이고 진실이다.

　실제로 남에게 속내를 드러내고 싶지 않은 지식인들이나 객관적인 글쓰기를 업(業)으로 삼고 있는 학자들에게 시라는 글쓰기는 좀처럼 선택하지 않는 작업이다. 그리고 오랫동안 고민하여 준비하지 않고는 그렇게 신속하게 작업을 진행하기는 쉽지 않은 일이다. 그렇기에 학자가 시인으로 등단하려는 결심을 하기까지 많은 고민이 있었을 것이라고 짐작했다. 또 나는 시인의 발 빠른 결단력과 추진력을 보면서 새삼 놀랐고, 지금까지 여러 자리에서 시인이 보여주었던 능력과 무관하지 않다는 사실도 깨달았다.

　내가 이런 사설을 앞세우는 이유는 시인의 시에서 언어를 분석하는 학자가 아니라 소리를 부리는 시인이라는 새로운 면모를 보았기 때문이다. 모름지기 시인이기 전에 한국어의 아름다움을 연구하고 가르치는 국어학자이자, 국어 선생이기에 문학적 수사를 동원하거나 낯선 표현을 써야 시가 된다는 것도 알고 있을 터인데, 시인의 시는 이런 가식적 표현이나 시적 기교와는 거리가 멀었다. 마치 가까운 가족이나 연인, 친구에게 자신의 이야기를 편하게 전하고 있는 것 같았다.

　구체적으로는 시인의 시가 화두(話頭)로 삼고 있는 것은 '친구', '꿈', '소리'였다. 시인은 집요하게 이 세 단어를 여러 맥락에서 풀어내고 있었으며, 이런 작업을 통해서 행복한 글쓰기를 실험하고 있었다. 나는 이런 작업들 속에서 고통스러운 글쓰기의 모습을 읽어내기보다는 순수하고 아름다운 추억을 뒤돌아보는 여행에 동행할 수 있었다. 그리고 시인의 여행 동반자였던 적이 몇 번 있었던 나에게 이런 추억 여행이 낯설지만은 않았다. 어떻든지 나는 시를 해설한다는 것이 사족(蛇足)에 지나지 않는다는 평범한 진리를 알고 있으면서도, 지금 시인의 이와 같은 시에 대해서 해설을 덧붙이고 있다.

2

이 세상에서 만난 사람들에게서 좋은 기억만을 가질 수는 없다. 혼자서는 감당하기 어려운 아픔을 남기고 떠나간 사람도 있고, 살아가는 순간마다에 나타나 훼방만을 놓았던 사람도 있다. 세상을 살면서 앞으로는 영원히 만나지 않았으면 사람도 있다. 그러나 시인은 이런 사람보다는 소중하고 아름다운 기억을 남겨주었던 사람들을 이야기하고 있다. 그 사람은 친구, 연인, 귀여운 사람 등으로 추억되고 있으며, 이들과의 행복한 시절의 꿈을 정겹고, 아름답고, 살갑고, 사랑스러운 모습으로 기록하고 있다.

이 같은 시인의 모색은 이 시집 전체에서 나타나고 있지만, 제1부 '친구와 함께'를 관통하는 주제이다. 시적 언어보다는 일상의 언어를 구사하여 나의 이야기, 친구의 이야기를 활자화하고 있다. 아름다운 꿈을 간직하고, 그 꿈을 먹고 살고자 하는 문학소녀의 치기를 보여주기도 하는 이와 같은 시적 글쓰기가 문학이 고급스러운 언어 예술만이 아니라 우리네 삶의 이야기를 진솔하게 전하고자 하는 정겨운 말 걸기라는 문학관으로도 설명할 수 있다. 즉 자신의 일상생활의 이야기를 자신의 목소리로 진솔하게 표현하는 것이라는 문학 생활화를 실천적으로 보여주고 있다. 이제 이런 시적 모색이 나타난 시구를 보도록 하자.

그러나 꿈이 많은 친구를 만나면
언제나 행복한 친구가 생각난다

꿈이 많아 행복한 친구
행복으로 꿈을 꾸는 친구

——「언제나 행복한 친구」 부분

함께 꿈꾸던 내 친구는
어느새 일어나 새 친구 찾았네

나 혼자 꿈속에 남아 있네
꿈속에서 또 다시 꿈을 꾸네

친구 떠난 꿈속에서
친구를 찾고 있네
뱅글뱅글 돌면서 꿈 친구 찾고 있네

— 「꿈을 꾸는 친구」 부분

　굳이 어려운 해설이 필요하지 않은 시구들이다. 시인은 항상 자신을 기쁘게 했던, 행복한 추억으로 기억되는 친구를 떠올리고 있다. 이처럼 시인에게 친구를 떠올리는 일은 행복한 꿈꾸기이다. 그리고 시인이 꿈속에서 애써 찾고 있는 행복한 친구는 시인 자신이기도 하다. 시적 화자인 '나'와 친구는 어느 순간 동일시되어 행복한 꿈꾸기에 동참하고 있다. 그래서 자신으로부터 멀리 떠나간 친구마저도 아름다운 기억으로 되살아날 수 있었으며, 시인의 행복한 꿈꾸기는 즐거운 항해를 계속할 수 있었다.

　본래 꿈의 속성이 그렇지만 시인은 꿈꾸기를 행복하거나 즐거운 것으로 기억하고자 한다. 그러나 이런 친구와의 만남이 때로는 인연이 아니었거나(「인연은 아니었는데…」) 소꿉놀이 친구(「친구」)였기에 지금은 아련한 추억으로만 남아 있다. 어쩌다가 만난 친구에게 "자네는 변함이 없네"(「자네는 변함이 없네」)라고 위로로 되지 않는 말을 전하기도 한다. 시인의 이와 같은 자기만족 혹은 자기변명은 어느 순간에 진지한 되돌아보기를 통해서 냉혹한 현실의 도전을 받기도 한다.

> 떫은 생감의 진실을
> 입 안 가득 깨물며 되새기는
> 매섭고 냉혹하게 구겨진
> 벗어던진 거짓 외투 속에서
> 아프게 부서지는 안개 속 부딪힘
>
> 거칠고 힘겨운 우리네 집짓기는
> 제비새끼 한 마리에 목숨을 건다
>
> ―「정(情)」 부분

　꿈속에서의 아름다운 추억이나 행복한 기억은 냉혹한 현실과는 너무나 다르다. 또 진실은 거짓의 외투를 벗고서야 만날 수 있는 것이며, '우리네' 삶은 크고 대단한 것이 아니라 사소한 일상의 것에 있음을 발견하고 있다. 이제 시인은 행복한 꿈꾸기에서 깨어나 진정한 자신을 찾아가는 여행을 시작하게 된다.

3

시인의 시선은 떠나간 친구를 추억하는 행복한 꿈꾸기에서 현실로 옮겨가고 있다. 이를 통해서 시인은 자신으로부터 멀어져간 사람보다는 자연의 소리에서 순수의 세계를 발견하게 된다. 이 세계는 '소리'라는 매개체를 통하여 인간의 이야기를 들려준다. 다른 사물이나 대상을 빌어 사람들의 이야기를 전하는, 소위 전경후정(前景後情)이라는 서정시의 미학이다. 그러나 시인은 이런 시적 기법을 의도적으로 구사하지는 않았다. 오히려 자연의 소리를 빌어 심혼(心魂)의 울림을 자연스럽게 담아내었다.

한국어를 학문의 연구 대상으로 삼고 있는 학자의 면모를 조금이라도 엿볼 수 있는 이 시들은 제2부 '소리따라 모양따라'에 묶여져 있다. 이 시들은 시가 소리를 운용하여 표현하는 문학이자 예술이라는 특성을 잘 보여준다. 그 소리는 시인이 일상에서 만나는 소리이며, 시인은 이 소리의 의미를 찾아내고, 사람살이와 관련시켜 그 의미를 풀어내고 있다. 예를 들면, 만남과 헤어짐, 행복한 어린 시절, 정겨운 사연 등과 같은 사소하기까지 한 우리네 삶을 꾸밈없는 이야기로 풀어내고 있다.

얼룩진 마음에 스며들고
새벽녘 귓가에 파고들고

바랜 가슴 위를
바퀴 따라 굴러가는
우리네 속삭임은
살금살금 반갑게 다가온다

—「소리」 부분

타닥 따다닥 타닥
부딪혀 떨어지는 빗소리에 새벽이 깬다

오늘은 친구가 떠나는 날

새벽을 깨우는 빗소리에
새벽잠 많은 친구 생각에
잠이 없는 하루를 시작한다

—「새벽을 깨우는 빗소리」 부분

반복과 대구, 의태어, 의성어 등이 자유자재로 구사되고 있는 이 시들은 시가 소리와 글자의 모양을 통하여 리듬을 실현하는 문학 갈래라는 사실을 확인시켜주고 있다. 그리고 이를 통해서 '우리네'의 이야기를 들려주고 있다. 그 이야기는 특별한 것이 아니라 조금만 눈을 돌려도 쉽게 만날 수 있는 것이며, 화려한 장식이나 수사가 필요하지 않은 순수를 간직한 것들이다. 따라서 시인의 시는 현학과는 거리가 멀다. 아름다운 우리

말의 소리를 엮어서 이런저런 이야기를 하고 있을 뿐이다.

'소리'에 대한 시인의 탐구는 비, 바람, 눈과 같은 자연에 관계된 것들이며, 우리 인간이 이 자연을 어떻게 바라보고 있는가를 이야기하고 있다. 그리고 시인이 자연을 빌어 들려주는 이야기는 순진무구의 세계다. 이런 시에서 시인은 "눈사람 만들던 민이/ 눈싸움 잘하던 진이/ 눈을 닮아 하얀 친구"(「눈 오리」)들을 추억하고 있다. 어찌 보면 앞의 시들에서 보았던 행복한 꿈꾸기와 별로 다르지 않다고 할 수 있는 이 같은 시 세계는 세상과 사람살이의 이야기를 소리로 치환하여 보여주었다는 점에서 차이가 있다. 이런 점은 다음과 같은 시에서도 나타난다.

사뿐히 내려앉은 봄 눈

겨울이 아쉬워
새 봄이 그리워

하얗게 하얗게
내려앉으며

내가 사온
수채화 물감처럼

멀리 저 멀리 흩날리고 있다

—「봄 눈」부분

일반적으로 '봄 눈'은 냉혹한 겨울을 보내고 따뜻한 봄을 맞는 서설(瑞雪)이다. 이 시에서 시인은 이 봄 눈을 보면서 가는 겨울을 아쉬워하고, 오는 봄을 그리워하는 복잡한 심정을 드러내고 있으며, "하얗게 하얗게"라는 표현을 통해서 봄 눈 내리는 모습을 소리로 형상화하고 있다. 또 시인이 지향하는 세계는 고요한("사뿐히 내려앉은"), 순박한("수채화 물감") 것임을 강조하고 있으며, 시인은 이런 세계를 촉각, 시각과 같은 감각적 이미지를 함축하고 환기하는 소리로 표현하고 있다.

4

친구와 꿈, 소리에 대한 모색을 보여주었던 시인의 시 세계는 소리를 찾아 떠나는 여행 시편으로 이어지고 있다. 이 시집의 제3부 '시간과 공간을 넘어'에 묶인 시들이 그 예이다. 이 시들은 비교적 오랜 기간에 걸쳐 쓰인 것으로 짐작된다. 그런 만큼 시·공간의 편폭(篇幅)도 크고, 그 시적 깊이나 내용의 편차도 크다. 대체로 여행 시편이 가지고 있는 사사로운 일상의 기록이라는 특성도 보인다. 그럼에도 불구하고 앞에서 살펴보았던 시 세계로부터 크게 벗어나지 않았다.

> 널려 널려 잘 익은 노란 자두를
> 하나, 둘, 다섯
>
> 그저 오르고
> 그저 깨물며
> 아이는 상큼한 눈웃음을
>
> ―「어느 날」부분

> 산 속에서 보내는 한적한 오후
> 나무 향기 풀 향기
> 꽃 향기 가득한 산 속에서
>
> 삐르륵 또록 컥컥 또로록 쫑쫑
> 또르르르 뻐뻐꾹 뻐꾹
>
> 산새들 노랫소리를 듣는다
>
> ―「산 속에서」부분

이처럼 시인은 여행 시편을 통해서도 순수의 세계를 소리로 표현하고 있다. 순박한 영혼, 훼손되지 않은 순수한 마음 세계를 노래하고 있다. 그 방식은 다른 시인들의 현란한 수사나 기교와는 거리가 멀었다. 소리의 본질과 특성을 알고 있는, 그리고 소리를 부릴 줄 아는 시인의 소박하고 일상적인 글쓰기였다. 그렇기에 이와 같은 시적 실험은 소리의 미학인 시에 대한 진정한 도전이라고도 평가할 수 있다.

어떻든지 나는 신현숙 시인의 일상적 글쓰기의 결과물들을 읽으면서 우리 시의 지향점을 다시 생각할 수 있었다. 특히 시가 어렵지 않다는 것, 어렵다는 것이 시의 미덕이 아니라는 사실을 새삼 되새길 수 있었다.

The Life-Telling World of 'Sound'

Yoon Yeo-Tak

(Literary Critic, Professor of Seoul National University)

1

Should I have the right to choose what to write about, one of the things I try to avoid is writing about the work of someone I know well. One day, however, I had received an e-mail and a phone call from poet Shin Hyon-Sook asking about publishing a collection of poems. I replied by saying that it is not difficult to publish a collection of one's own poems, noting that publishing is one of the numerous ways for one to become a poet. Within a few days, I was offering some advice and guidance on poetry publishing. It was not too long after that I had a typeset collection of poems delivered to me. Such series of events took place very rapidly. Within the process, I congratulated the birth of a new poet, and I was asked to write a commentary about the soon-to-be-published collection of poems. This kind of dream-like story is both a fact and a truth.

For intellectuals who do not like to expose their inner feelings or for scholars who treat objective writing as a trade, poetry writing is not a profession that is chosen so readily. Also, without any painstaking effort and preparation, it is not a task that can be so easily executed. It is my assumption that a lot of concerns would have been attached to a scholar's ultimate decision to make a debut as a poet. Furthermore, I was stunned by the poet's nimble-footed decisive action and drive, dawning on me that the capabilities revealed by this poet on various occasions up to now are not coincidental.

The reason I went ahead with this commentary is because the poetry comes not from a scholar who analyzes language but rather illustrates a new countenance to poetry where a poet manages sound.

It may have been easy to perceive this poet simply as a linguist, who studies and teaches the beauty of the Korean language. As a language teacher, she also most certainly would have been aware that a poem is formed with figures of speech or by using uncommon expressions. But this poet's poetry is as far as far can be from such tangible expressions and poetic techniques. Rather, the poems felt like she was comfortably sharing her personal stories to her close family members, significant other, or friends.

Specifically, the topics embraced by the poet's poems were "friend," "dream," and "sound."

As the poet tenaciously unraveled these three words in various contexts, I was able to through such process experiment with pleasurable writing. Rather than perceiving a tormenting writing process through each piece, it felt like I was accompanying the poet through her pure and beautiful journey down memory lane. Also, having been one of the poet's travel companions a number of times, such a trip down memory lane was not all that unfamiliar. Although I am aware by plain principle that my comments about poetry should be free of unnecessary comments, I know I am doing that just now about this poet's poetry.

2

It is not possible to have only good memories of the people we meet in this world. There are people who pass on leaving a pain that was difficult to bear alone, and there are people who only cause disruptions throughout life's journey. We also encounter throughout our lives people whom we never want to meet again. Instead of these kinds of people, the poet talks of those people who gave her a precious and beautiful memory. These people encompass a friend, a lover, and a cute person, among others, who are memorable. The poet records the dreams of such happy times with these people in a warm, beautiful, tender, and endearing way.

Such renditions can be found in the whole collection of poems, but the permeating theme is of "With a Friend" found in Part 1. Rather than with poetic language, the poet uses everyday prosaic language to depict her personal story and her friend's story. The poet illustrates how she had treasured the beauty of her youthful dream, and that young girl's aims to consume and live that dream. Such poetic penmanship can be described as literature being not only a sophisticated form of linguistic art, but also as an affectionate dialogue expressing our life story in an honest and sincere way. For instance, the compositions display, in a practical style, the poet sincerely telling the story of her everyday life through her own voice. Let us now look at the verses harboring these kinds of poetic illustrations.

But when I meet a friend full of dreams
I always think of a happy friend

A friend happy from being full of dreams
A friend who dreams out of happiness

Excerpt from: Always a Happy Friend

Hey my friend with whom I had shared my dreams
One day got up and found a new friend

Hey now I'm left alone in the dream

I'm dreaming again in my sleep

Hey in the dream where my friend has left me
I'm looking for a friend
Going around and around I'm looking for a dream friend

Excerpt from: A Dreaming Friend

These are verses that do not require a complex commentary.

The poet conjures up a friend who always made her happy and is remembered as a happy memory. As such, bringing back to mind a friend is like having a happy dream. Also, this happy friend the poet labors to find in her dreams is the poet herself. The narrator, "me," and the friend at some point become equal, participating in the act of dreaming happily. As a result, the narrator is able to revive the long-departed friend as a beautiful memory, while continuing the joyful voyage of dreaming happily.

Although such is the nature of a dream, the poet seeks to remember dreaming as something happy and joyful. However, the meeting with a friend was, at times, not meant to be (It Wasn't Destiny⋯), or remained only as a distant memory because it was of a childhood friendship (Friend). To a friend encountered once in a while, the poet conveys less affectionate words such as "you haven't changed" (You Haven't Changed). Through the act of seriously looking back, such expressions of self-satisfaction or self-justification suddenly become a challenge of the harsh reality.

> The truth of the unripe persimmon
> In a mouthful is chewed over and over
> In the severely and cruelly crinkled

Fake overcoat that is thrown away
Collides within the fog painfully giving way

Building our rugged and beleaguered home
Is like having a baby swallow's life on the line

Excerpt from: Tender Feelings

The beautiful memories and the joyful recollections inside the dream are very different from the harsh realities. Furthermore, the truth can only be met once the fake overcoat is removed, "our" life is not something that is large and great but discovering that it exists in our simple everyday lives. Now awakened from dreaming happily, the poet begins her journey of true self discovery.

3

The poet's eyes shift to reality from dreaming happily about the memories of the long-departed friend. Through this process, the poet, as opposed to being a person who has grown distant from oneself, is able to discover the genuine world from the sound of nature. This world tells the story of humanity through the medium of "sound." It is a form of the so-called "foreground 'backaffection'" 전경후정(前景後情), the aesthetics of lyric poems conveying people's stories through another object or subject.

The poet, however, did not deliberately use such poetic techniques. Rather, she naturally captured the heart and soul of the reverberations from the sound of nature. The poems that provide at least a small glimpse of the countenance of the scholar who embraces Korean language as a subject of study are tied together in Part 2: By Sound By Shape. By employing sound, these poems effectively show the expressive nature of literature and art. These sounds are the very sounds the poet encounters in everyday life, prompting her to find meaning in the sounds and unravel the meaning in relation to people's lives. For example, the poet deduces such instances as meeting and separation, a happy childhood, nostalgia, and even trivial aspects of our lives in a straightforward manner.

> Our whispers
> Soaked into my stained heart
> Penetrated in my ear in the peak of dawn
> As if rolling in the heels of a tire

Over my washed-out heart
Stealthily and delightedly draw near

Excerpt from: Sound

Plip plip ploop ploop
Dawn awakes in the colliding raindrops
Today is the day of my friend's departure

With the sound of the rain awaking dawn
In the thought of my sleepyhead friend
I start my sleepless day

Excerpt from: The Sound of Rain Waking Dawn

The poetic works freely apply repetition and rhyming couplets, mimetic words, and onomatopoeic words, underscoring the fact that the poems are a literary offshoot that achieves rhythm through sound and the shape of the letters. And through such means, the poet tells about "our" stories. These stories are not special but ones that would easily catch our eyes with a little attention, thus reinforcing how purity is cherished by not resorting to ornate language and figure of speech. Consequently, the poet's works are distant from pedantry. She is simply telling stories of this and that by interweaving the beauty of the sounds of the Korean language.

As the poet's exploration of "sound" is related to elements of nature such as rain, wind, and snow, she is telling about how humanity views nature. Furthermore, the stories told through nature are a world of naivety. For example, in "Snow Duck," the poet is reminiscing about "Minnie who had made snowmen/ Jinnie who had been good at snowball fighting/ A white friend like snow" (2-4). Such kind of poetry world, which does not seem to be that different from the dreaming happily theme seen in earlier poems, is different in that it has shown the stories of the world and everyday living in substitution with sound.

The spring snow falling lightly

Winter is being missed
Spring is being longed for

In white in white
Drifting down

They flutter about far far away
Like the watercolors
I have bought.

Excerpt from: Spring Snow

Generally, "Spring Snow" is auspicious snow signaling the coming of the warm spring and the letting go of the harsh cold winter. In this poem, the poet is lamenting the drifting away of winter while gazing at the spring snow. At the same time, the poet is expressing a mixture of feelings as she yearns for spring. And through the "In white in white" expression, the image of snow falling is expressed into sound. In addition, the world the poet illustrates is being emphasized as tranquil ("The spring snow falling lightly"), and simple ("Like the watercolors"). The poet is illustrating such world by implying such sensuous images as touch and sight and through arousing sound.

4

The world inside the poems that depicted the poet seeking for her friend, dreams, and sound continues onto a chapter of poems about a departure journey while in search of sound. Examples of this are precisely those poems in Part 3, "Beyond Time and Space," of this collection of poems. It appears as though that these compositions were completed relatively over a longer period of time. As such, the area of the poems is larger, while the poetic depth and content range are greater as well. On the whole, the travel poems can be characterized as recordings of the trivial matters of everyday life. Despite all this, the world inside the poems does not deviate much from that seen in the earlier poems.

The scattered scattered well-ripened yellow plums
One, two, five

Just climbing
Just biting
The child with refreshing smiling eyes

Excerpt from: One Day

A quiet afternoon in the mountains
Tree scent grass scent
In the mountains filled with the scent of flowers

Chirrup cheep chirp chirrup chirp
Chirrup cheep chirp

Listening to the singing of the mountain birds

Excerpt from: In the Mountains

Even through the travel-poem collection, the poet delineates the pure world through sound. The poems sing about a world of the simple soul and the untarnished pure heart. Such style is far removed from the ornate figure of speech and technique exhibited by other poets. These poems are the simple everyday writings of the poet who not only understands the intrinsic nature and characteristics of sound, but also has a strong command over it. Such poetic experimentation can be assessed as showing a genuine challenge to create aesthetic poems of sound.

In any case, reading the product of poet Shin Hyon-Sook's everyday routine writing made me rethink about the current purpose of our poems. More significantly, I was able to realize that poetry is not complex and confirm that complexity is not a virtue of poems.